The MattieJ Pocketbook Reference Guide

Author: **Donna T. Brown**

Illustrator: **Jake Robbins**

February 2023

Some characters and events in this
book are fictitious,
Any similarity to real persons, living
or dead, is coincidental and
not intended by the author.

ACKNOWLEDGEMENTS

To my husband and life partner in ministry Jimmy "Boom Boom" Brown, Sr...
I am forever yours! After 32 years of marriage, your love and support is supreme.
I appreciate you for that. Above all else, thank you for allowing me to roam free in
who I am to you, God and the Universe.

To my children Teryl (Curtisha), Jimmy Jr. (Sonni), and Autumn Faith...all I will ever
desire to do is to make you guys proud. Thank you for sharing your thoughts, input
and wisdom with me...I LISTENED! Love you muchly.

To my newfound and loyal Sister-friend, Author and Poet Velda Boyland Austin
of Memphis, TN...thank you for your knowledge, hard work, and weekly
commitment in making sure this project was executed successfully. I am eternally
grateful to you for every sacrifice made.

Finally, to my Publics...the group of individuals who make my day EVERYDAY.
I can't explain the honor I feel to be chosen to be your source of comedy relief.
Thank you for "tuning in" to the madness and making it a joy to entertain each
of you.

FOREWORD

The MattieJ Pocketbook Reference Guide is a mini-manual that allows
interested viewers to better understand the wacky world of MattieJ.
It's merely the beginning of what's to come as it relates to publications
from MattieJ's Ministry of Laughter.

DEDICATIONS

This book is dedicated to the memory of my loved ones
who are not physically present
with me but, their spirits are constant. My Grandmother Bertha Patterson,
Father Roy Lee Thomas, Mother Janie P. Thomas and
last but not least, my beautiful
sister Letitia Ann Thomas who was my very first fan and inspiration.

SPECIAL DEDICATION TO GOD

I am eternally grateful to God for choosing me to be his pharmacist for laughter.
In turn I have vowed to dispense it daily in large doses.

Proverbs 17:22

MattieJ's Bio

MattieJ is a no-nonsense, quick-witted elderly lady who tells it like it is.
She is married to her mild-mannered husband Herman and together they
take on the small close knit community and the shenanigans are
never-ending. The Witherspoons are prominent leaders in their local
church and community. Herman is the Chairman of the Deacon's Board
and MattieJ is the President of the Usher's Board. Between MattieJ's weekly
church suspensions and arrest activity, there is rarely a quiet moment in
their family, church and community.

MattieJ's Antics

- MattieJ communicates with her "Publics" via Social Media.
- When Herman is nearby, she will lean into the corner of the screen to whisper to her Publics.
- No one in MattieJ's circle or community can put up their Christmas Tree until Mattie releases Christmas. Otherwise, she will do what she calls a "tuck and roll" in your front yard.
- Don't speak to, hug on, or laugh with Herman.
- MattieJ's ushers must have a criminal background.
- Mattie can talk about Herman, but no one else can or there will be a fight.
- MattieJ normally "Blacks Out" before she jumps on somebody.
- MattieJ never starts fights, she ends them.
- MattieJ uses 2 knives. The one she cuts with and the one she guts with.

QUOTES

- "Herman is moderate" - this means that Herman is easygoing.

- "Before I knowed it" - "Before I knew it." This saying is usually prefaced before an "incidental."

- "You think I didn't when I did?"

- "The Devil issa lie and His wife" (does whatever Mattie says she does).

- "U say Sum?" "Did you say something?" Normally addressed to Herman.

- Hollin' N Screamin' N Screamin' N Hollin' - explanation of high emotions.

- "And thangs like that" and other similar things.

- "And so"...what Mattie says when she's continuing her conversation.

- "Tender towards me" - the act of feeling "kind and sweet" towards Mattie.

- "Help Me Jesus, Help me Lawd" - an expression MattieJ uses when she's in trouble.

Some of the Characters in MattieJ's World

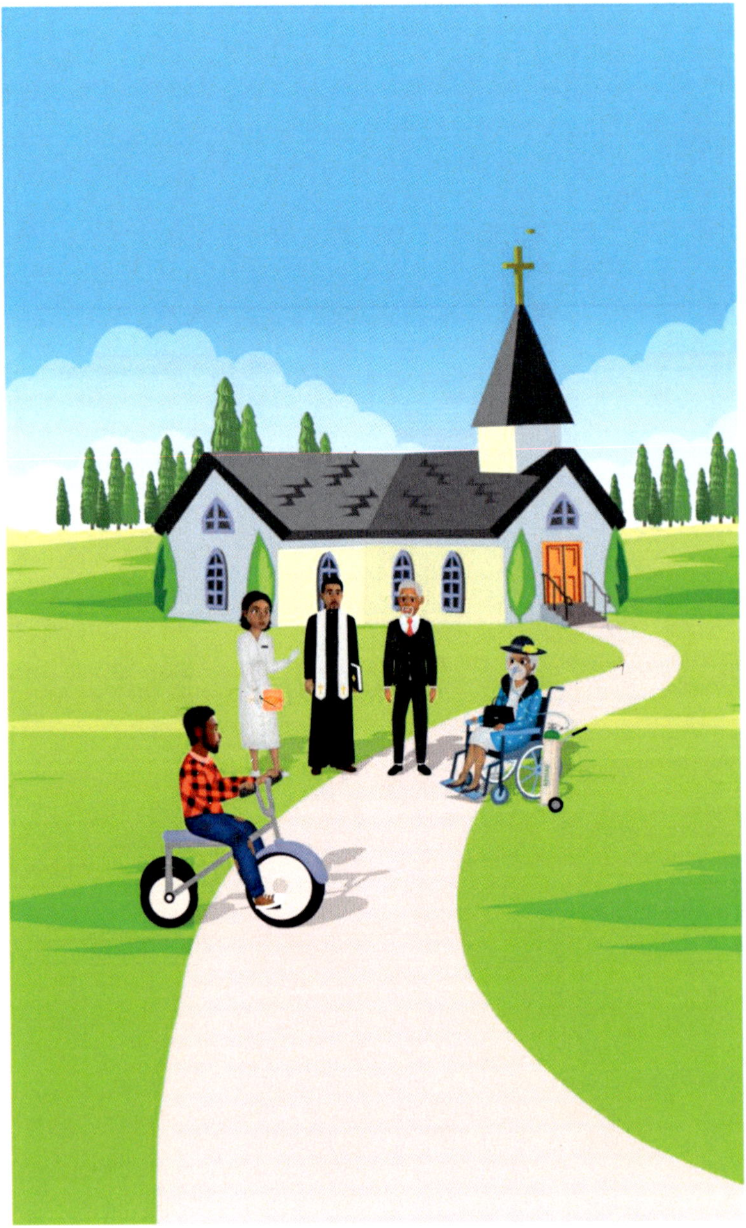

CHARACTERS

MattieJ - an old school, quick-witted and hilariously funny housewife who is in constant trouble with her church, the law and most of her family members and friends.

Herman - MattieJ's loving and devoted husband who does his very best to keep his wife on the straight and narrow path.

Mattie's Siblings - Lily Ruth, Electa, Fletchie, Roosevelt

Roosevelts Ugly Grandchildren - Mick Jaquar, Glow N the Dark, and Umbilical Cord

Herman's Siblings - Memphis, Lollipop, LC and Ruby Jean

Ushers - Florine, DelFrankie, Matilda, Margarite, Mae Ethel and Bobbie Ann

Deacons - Threadgill, Porterfield, Hale, Herman and the nameless one who MattieJ refers to as the deacon who wears all 3 pcs. of his suits.

Popcone - MattieJ's friend who also attends church with MattieJ. Popcone is 38 yrs. old and drives a tricycle to church. Mattie is very protective of Popcone.

Cassie - Popcone's mother

Craig Lee - Popcone's best friend who attends MattieJ's church

Big Jake Early - MattieJ's redneck ex-boyfriend.

Big Fine Pearlie Mae - Pearlie Mae is known for her beautiful figure as well as her beautiful voice. Mattie suspects that she and Herman had some hanky panky going on.

Gilbert Ray/Mildred - Gilbert Ray is the local meat man. Mildred is his wife.

Cash Money - MattieJ's "ratchet" grand daughter-in-law and hair stylist.

Shawt Change - Cash Money's "ratchet" mother

Petey Boi - MattieJ's grandson who use to help her do drive-bys

Sugarfoot and her Stanken Daughters - A mother and her smelly daughters who attends MattieJ's church.

Pastor - MattieJ's mild-mannered Pastor who has a fainting condition.

White Menz Attorneys - Scott and Big Dave are MattieJ's pro bono attorneys who have kept her out of jail for many years.

Randy - MattieJ's arresting officer. No one can arrest Mattie but Randy.

Verlene Jackson - Herman's Ex from Dallas County. Mattie detests her because of what she wrote in Herman's yearbook.

Mae Doris - one of MattieJ's simple-minded friends.

Shay Shay - MattieJ's niece and Lecta's granddaughter.

Squirrel - Herman's Best Friend.

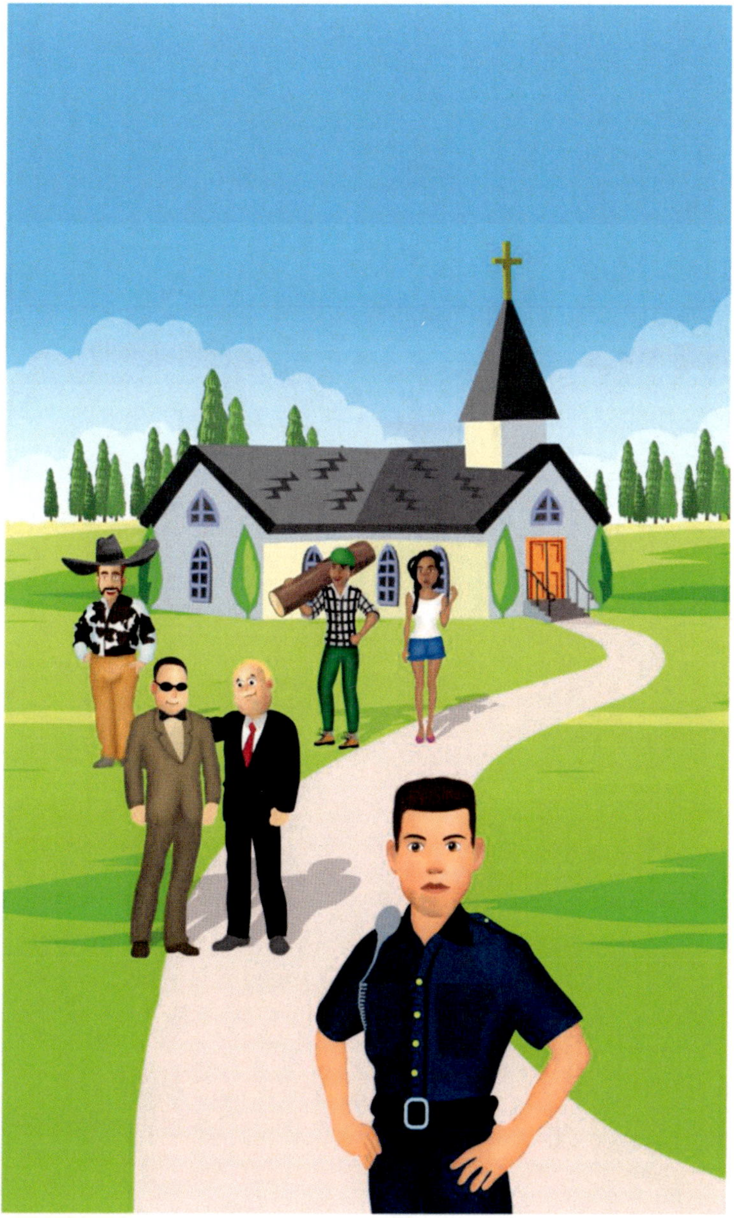

Some of MattieJ's Vocabulary Words

Aa

Africus Americus - African American

Anointment - to be anointed

Atall - at all

Bb

Bipolaroid - the state of being bipolar

Blocksation- the act of being blocked on Social Media

Bowlegged Suit - Herman's special suit that makes him appear bowlegged

Brang - to bring

Cc

Categorically - direct and absolute

Cerebellus - the cerebellum (Part of the brain)

Chirrens - children

Congestinal - to have congestion

Containment laughs - laughter that can be contained or held

Conversational - regarding conversation

Cose - coarse

Cosmopolitan license - cosmetology license

Crynin' - crying (to cry)

Dd

Deacon Bode • Deacon's Board

Direckly • directly/no changing or stopping

Ee

Esophacal Trail • pertaining to the Esophagus

Ff

Facebook TV - Facebook

Familiarity - the act of being familiar

Five Fold Ministry - Taken from Ephesians 4:11 but for Mattie, it's her 5 fingers folded to fight

Foots - feet

Fune - funeral

Hh

Heifa - a distasteful, classless, shady woman

Helfa-at-hand - the subject heifa. The heifa MattieJ is referring to

Heifarocity - the act of being a Heifa

Heifarism - to conduct yourself in the way of a Heifa

Horspilla - the hospital

Ii

Identificationals - items used to identify an individual

Ignunt/Ignunce - to be ignorant

Incidentals - an event of occurrences that normally results in violence on MattieJ's end

Kk

Killation - the act of being killed

Ll

Level To Level - straight talk

Locality - your location

Locomotive blows - a punch style of Mattie's with the strength comparable to a locomotive

Mm

Medullus - medulla oblongata (a part of the brain)

Mens - Men

Mustyness - the state of being musty

Oo

Orientus - Oriental

Pp

Particula' - to be subpar in intelligence

Peoples - people

Pivotal blows - rotating punches

Prexactly - precisely mixed with exactly

Public - MattieJ's loyal followers

Puerto Reefus - Puerto Rican

Qq

Qwershton - question

Rr

Repote - report

Ss

Scholarshift - scholarship

Sequence - the order of things according to MattieJ

Skress n skrain - stress and strain

Spetifically - specifically

Stewpit - stupid

Suspectical - of being a suspect

Tt

Texas message - text message

Tuck n roll - a tactical landing used by MattieJ when exiting a vehicle

Uu

Uniformity - to be as one/in unison

Upgraced - to upgrade

Upsot - the act of being upset

Usha Bode - Usher's Board

Ushaship - the state of being an usher

Vv

Velocity - the speed of MattieJ's punches

Ww

Whoopsation - the act of being whooped up by MattieJ

Womenz - women

Yy

Yestiddy - yesterday

Social Media Platforms and Contact Information

Brown Ministries
P.O. Box 316 Chelsea, AL
35043,
205-568-2861
Brownministriesinc2018@gmail.com

FACEBOOK
Youtube: MattieJ and MattieJ LIVE

TikTok: mrsmattie

IG: mrs.mattiej

Made in the USA
Monee, IL
20 April 2023